CREATIVE ⦁ EDUCATION

ATLANTA

NL WEST

BRAVES

41

MICHAEL E. GOODMAN

Published by Creative Education, Inc.
123 S. Broad Street, Mankato, Minnesota 56001

Art Director, Rita Marshall
Cover and title page design by Virginia Evans
Cover and title page illustration by Rob Day
Type set by FinalCopy Electronic Publishing
Book design by Rita Marshall

Photos by Allsport, Duomo, Focus on Sports,
Spectra-Action, Sportschrome, Sports Illustrated,
UPI/Bettmann and Wide World Photos

Copyright © 1992 Creative Education, Inc.
International copyrights reserved in all countries.
No part of this book may be reproduced in any form
without written permission from the publisher.
Printed in the United States of America.

Library of Congress Cataloging-in-Publication Data

Goodman, Michael E.
  Atlanta Braves / by Michael E. Goodman.
  p. cm.
  Summary: A team history of an old and traveled
baseball team, whose early winning record has never
been topped. Hightlights former and present players
such as Hank Aaron and Dale Murphy.
  ISBN 0-88682-460-5
  1. Atlanta Braves (Baseball team)—History—
Juvenile literature.   [1. Atlanta Braves (Baseball
team)—History.   2. Baseball—History.]   I. Title.
GV875.A8G66 1991   91-10384
796.357'64'09758231—dc20   CIP

THE HOME OF THE BRAVES

The southern part of the United States has a reputation for being quiet and slow-moving. This is not true of Atlanta, Georgia, however, which is a bustling and exciting place. It is the business center of the South, boasting the largest airport in the world and some of the worst traffic jams anywhere during rush hour every weekday morning.

There is also nothing slow-moving about Atlanta-Fulton County Stadium, the home of the Atlanta Braves. The stadium is sometimes called "the launching pad" because of all of the home runs that get blasted over its outfield walls every baseball season.

Atlanta is the focal point of baseball in the South. Fans throughout the southeastern United States follow the

Atlanta pitcher Tom Glavine.

exploits of the Atlanta Braves. They haven't always had great teams to cheer for—the Atlanta Braves have not made it to a World Series yet. But since the Braves moved to Atlanta from Milwaukee in 1966, southern baseball fans have had some great players and great moments to remember: Phil Niekro's no-hitter against the San Diego Padres in August 1973, Hank Aaron's record-breaking 715th home run in April 1974, Dale Murphy's back-to-back Most Valuable Player awards in 1982 and 1983, and more.

Today's Braves are still struggling to reach the top of the National League. But, like Atlanta, the team is young and growing, and the future is bright.

The long tradition of the Braves began in Boston, the team was called the Red Stockings.

FROM FIRST TO LAST TO FIRST AGAIN

While the Braves haven't always been a top squad, they began their long history as the most dominant team in baseball. This was during the early 1870s, when the team played its home games in Boston, Massachusetts, and was known as the Red Stockings. Boston won four consecutive championships in the first professional league in baseball history, the National Association of Professional Base Ball Players. Then, in 1876, the National Association was disbanded because there was too much cheating and gambling on games.

Baseball fans in Boston were angry. They didn't want to lose their major league franchise, and luckily they didn't. Soon Boston joined with teams from seven other cities to form a new organization, the National League.

Phil Niekro.

1 9 0 1

Kid Nichols won 20 games as a pitcher and also played the outfield and first base.

The team that began as the Boston Red Stockings and is now known as the Atlanta Braves has played in the National League every year since 1876.

Between 1876 and 1900, Boston captured eight National League titles under such nicknames as the Red Caps, Beaneaters, Nationals, Doves, and Rustlers. (The name Braves didn't become official until 1912.) The best player in those years was pitcher Charles "Kid" Nichols. During the 1890s, Nichols recorded thirty or more victories in seven different seasons, finishing his career with 362 wins, sixth best in baseball history.

By 1901, Kid Nichols was gone, however, and so were the Boston team's winning ways. Between 1900 and 1913, Boston finished seventh three times and eighth five times in the eight-team National League. And if you were asked to guess where the Braves would finish at the end of the 1914 season, you would have said, "Dead last"— unless you believed in miracles.

Boston manager George Stallings was such a believer. When Stallings first was named to head the Braves in 1912, he turned to the team's owner and said, "I've been stuck with some terrible teams in my day, but this one beats them all!"

Then Stallings went to work to change things. He made trade after trade, looking for new talent. He also drove his players mercilessly, shouting his motto: "You can win. You must win. You will win!"

Stallings was certain the team was ready to make its move in 1914. Unfortunately, for the first half of the season, that move was downward. On July 4, the Braves were in last place, fifteen games behind the front-running New York Giants. Injuries and bad luck plagued the Braves. Things were so bad that the team even lost an exhibition game to a soap company squad.

Still, Stallings didn't give up. He made his players arrive at the ballpark hours before each game for early morning chalkboard sessions. The players learned their lessons well and then began putting them to work. They won game after game as they rose from last place to first in only five weeks. Once they caught up with the Giants, the Braves just kept on going. In all, the team captured fifty-two of its final sixty-six games that year and finished the season a whopping ten and a half games in front of New York.

Then came the World Series. The inexperienced Braves were pitted against Connie Mack's Philadelphia Athletics, world champs in three of the previous four years. Everyone expected the Braves' miracle season to end quickly, except George Stallings. He reminded his players of his motto before game one, and the Braves stormed to a 7–1 win. Game two was a scoreless struggle until the Braves tallied a ninth-inning run for the victory. The Athletics and their fans were stunned.

In game three, the Braves pushed across the winning run in the bottom of the twelfth inning. They completed their improbable four-game sweep the next day.

Thirty-six years later, the country's sportswriters were asked to pick the greatest baseball upset of the first fifty years of the twentieth century. The "Miracle Braves" of 1914 won, hands down.

1 9 1 4

Catcher Hank Gowdy led the Braves with an incredible .545 average during the World Series.

9

Trying to create another miracle, outfielder Oddibe McDowell.

Second baseman Jeff Treadway.

1 9 4 2

Warren Spahn (right) appeared in a Braves' uniform for the first time; his career would ultimately span 22 years.

SPAHN SPINS THE BRAVES TO THE TOP

George Stallings and the Braves ran out of miracles after 1914. Boston didn't reach the World Series again for thirty-four years. Instead, the team plunged back toward the bottom of the National League, finishing in fifth place or lower more than half of those years. Things began to change, however, with the arrival of a tall, thin lefthander from Buffalo, New York, named Warren Spahn.

Between 1947 and 1964, Spahn was the mainstay of the Braves pitching staff, first in Boston and then in Milwaukee (where the team moved in 1953). Braves fans could always count on him. "Spahn hated to miss a turn," a teammate once said. "He expected to pitch every fourth day no matter what. He loved baseball and he loved to pitch; you got the feeling sometimes that pitching was his whole life."

Spahn had a fine pitching mind as well as a strong arm. Braves pitching coach Whit Wyatt once said, "Every pitch he throws has got an idea behind it. He is always a step ahead of the batter. And he knows how to find the corners of the plate better than anyone I've ever known."

That was the main idea behind Spahn's pitching strategy. "I never throw a ball down the middle of the plate," he said. "In fact, I ignore the twelve inches in the middle and concentrate on hitting the two and a half inches on each side or corner of it." That strategy drove National League batters crazy for nearly two decades and helped Spahn become the winningest lefthander in baseball history, with a record of 363 wins and 245 losses.

Spahn spent his first full year with the Braves in 1947, when he won twenty-one games and lost only ten. He teamed with righthander Johnny Sain to form the best one-two pitching combination in baseball. Unfortunately, the Braves didn't have much else on their pitching staff and counted on the duo to carry the load. Braves fans came up with a new slogan: "Spahn and Sain, and pray for rain."

The fans' prayers were answered in 1948. Together, Spahn and Sain drove the Braves to their first National League championship since 1914.

This time, there were no miracles, however. The Cleveland Indians roared past the Braves in six games in the 1948 World Series. Who recorded the two Braves victories during the series? Spahn and Sain, of course!

Even though the Braves had below-average records between 1949 and the mid-1950s, Warren Spahn

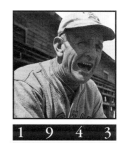

The legendary Casey Stengel managed his last of six Braves' teams.

1 9 5 3

Eddie Mathews became the first rookie in major league history to hit 3 home runs in a game.

remained the National League's most dominant pitcher. Spahn often had to earn his wins on his own in those years. His teammates never seemed to be able to score runs for him. He lost countless games by 1–0 or 2–1 scores, and many times he had to pitch shutouts in order to win.

Despite Spahn's heroics, the Braves' many losing seasons caused a big drop-off in attendance at games in Boston. Finally, the team's owner decided to move the franchise to Milwaukee, Wisconsin, in 1953. The move was a spectacular success. That first year, the Braves jumped from seventh place to second, and a National League record 1.8 million fans attended Braves games in Milwaukee.

Warren Spahn also had a big year, winning twenty-three games to top all league pitchers. He had help from a young righthander named Lew Burdette, who had replaced Johnny Sain as the team's number-two starter. For the first time in many years, the Braves also had a terrific power source—the electricity-charged bat of third baseman Eddie Mathews, who led all National League sluggers with forty-seven home runs. The Braves were on their way back to the top.

Warren Spahn's knack for winning big games was a major reason for the Braves' rise. (He had two of his best seasons in 1957 and 1958, when the Braves won their last two National League pennants.) His success was a combination of talent and desire. A Braves coach once said of him, "If there's one game you have to win, then you must go with Spahn. He's got the heart."

Derek Lilliquist follows in the giant footsteps of Warren Spahn.

"HAMMERIN' HANK" AARON LAUNCHES A NEW ERA

In his first season
with the Braves
Hank Aaron batted
.280 and slammed
13 homers.

Spahn and Burdette made a great pitching duo for the Braves in the early 1950s. Then Henry Aaron arrived in 1954 to join Eddie Mathews in the lineup. Soon the Braves also had the best one-two power punch in the National League.

Aaron decided early that he wanted to become a major league baseball player and began working toward his goal. "If Henry wasn't at home, you knew he was over at the park playing ball," his mother said. "That's all he ever wanted to do."

When he was eighteen, Aaron joined the Indianapolis Clowns team in the old Negro League. He was a short-stop in those days—and not a particularly good fielder. But could he hit! He was batting a whopping .467 for the Clowns and smacking tape-measure home runs when a Braves scout noticed him and signed him to a contract in 1952. No one could figure out where all of his power came from. He was skinny and not very muscular, but he had huge wrists that enabled him to whip the bat around with amazing speed. That was his secret.

"I turn my wrists over. My right hand turns over toward the pitcher so, when I hit the ball, there's a rotation on it that makes the ball go a long way," he explained. He soon earned the nickname "Hammerin' Hank."

The Braves sent Aaron to Puerto Rico to play winter ball and to learn a new position, the outfield. By 1954, twenty-year-old Aaron was in the major leagues as a backup outfielder.

During spring training of Aaron's rookie year, Braves outfielder Bobby Thomson broke an ankle sliding into a base. To everyone's surprise, manager Charlie Grimm threw Aaron a mitt and said, "Get in there, kid."

"All the breaks came my way that spring," Aaron said. But he had made himself ready for those breaks. "Because I had played winter ball to get outfield experience, I was in tiptop shape for playing," he noted. Young Aaron played so well that Bobby Thomson never got his starting spot back. For the next twenty-one years, Hank Aaron owned right field for the Braves.

Throughout his career Aaron remained shy and quiet. He let his bat do the talking. No bat had spoken as loudly or as consistently since the days of the immortal Babe Ruth of the Yankees. Year after year, Aaron hit between twenty-five and forty-five homers and drove in one hundred or more runs.

Aaron hit one of the most important home runs and scored two of his most important RBI on September 23, 1957, in Milwaukee. The Braves had been battling the St. Louis Cardinals all season for first place. They needed a win over the Cardinals on that day to clinch their first pennant since 1948. The tense battle went into the twelfth inning deadlocked at 2–2. Braves shortstop Johnny Logan led off the inning with a single. However, the next two batters made outs, and Logan was still standing on base. Up came Hank Aaron. He powered a Billy Moffett pitch high over the center field wall for his forty-third homer of the year, and the Braves were National League champs.

Aaron and his teammates kept right on going in the World Series against the favored Yankees. With Aaron slugging three homers, knocking in seven runs, and batting .393—and with Lew Burdette giving up just two

The legendary Hank Aaron (pages 18–19).   17

Hank Aaron (right) won the batting title, but the Braves lost the pennant on the last day of the season.

runs in three well-pitched victories—the Braves displaced the Yankees as world champs. It was the team's first time atop baseball's throne since the 1914 miracle.

Aaron had another super year in 1958, and the Braves won a second straight National League title. They jumped out to a lead of three games to one over the Yankees in the World Series, and then fell apart. The Yankees won the last three contests to regain their championship status.

That was the last time any Braves team won a National League pennant. No one really knows why Milwaukee slowly dropped out of contention, but Hank Aaron had a theory. "We were fat, rich, and spoiled," Aaron said later, recalling the seasons after 1958. "And the fans were spoiled, too."

The "spoiled" Milwaukee fans grew tired and impatient as the Braves dropped down in the standings over the next few years. Finally, in 1966, the team was moved for the second time in fourteen years. Its new home was more than eight hundred miles south, in Atlanta, Georgia.

In Atlanta, just as in Milwaukee, Hank Aaron hammered the ball with amazing consistency. He slowly began to creep up on Babe Ruth in the record books. On May 19, 1970, Aaron achieved something that not even the great Ruth ever had—he smacked his three thousandth hit. With that milestone, he became the first man in baseball history to get three thousand hits and five hundred home runs. (Only Willie Mays has matched that feat since.)

Next, Aaron took aim at Babe Ruth's career home run record. The pressure on Aaron became unbelievable as he closed in on Ruth. Aaron had never enjoyed being in the spotlight, but now he was really uncomfortable. "I'm not trying to replace Babe Ruth," he said, "I'm just trying to do my job."

Aaron entered the 1973 season forty-one home runs behind Ruth. On the next-to-the-last day of the year, the forty-year-old Aaron slammed homer number forty. On the last day, he got three hits—all singles. Ruth's record was safe for one more year . . . or at least one more game. In his very first time at bat in 1974, Aaron slammed home run number 714 to tie Ruth's record.

Four days later, one mighty swing against Dodger pitcher Al Downing made Henry Aaron baseball's all-time home run king. Hammerin' Hank was all business as he circled the bases, but inside his heart was pounding. "I don't remember the noise or the two kids that I'm told ran the bases with me. My teammates at home plate, I remember seeing them. I remember my mother out there

1 9 5 7

Called up from the minor leagues as a late season replacement, Bob "Hurricane" Hazle sparked Milwaukee to the pennant.

21

Another Atlanta slugger, Dale Murphy.

and her hugging me. That's what I remember more than anything else about the home run when I think back on it," he later recalled.

Braves relief pitcher Tom House grabbed the ball in the Braves bullpen after it went over the fence and raced toward home plate to hand it to Aaron. "I looked and he had tears hanging on his eyelids," House said. "I put the ball in his hand, and he touched me on the shoulder. It was then that it was brought home to me what this home run meant not only to him, but to all of us."

1 9 7 0

Rico Carty led the Braves and the National League in batting with a .366 average.

NIEKRO KNUCKLES OVER BRAVES OPPONENTS

During Hank Aaron's career with the Braves, he played with two of the finest pitchers in the franchise's history. Warren Spahn was the Braves' top pitcher when Aaron started with the Milwaukee Braves, and Phil Niekro was number one on the mound for the Atlanta Braves when Aaron retired.

The two hurlers had very different approaches to winning games, but both were successful. While Spahn threw hard and nicked corners with pinpoint control, Niekro threw the most frustrating, slow-moving knuckleball in the game. And no one, sometimes not even Niekro himself, knew just where wind currents would carry his fifty-mile-per-hour floaters. "I don't always know which way the ball is going to break," Niekro said, "particularly on a windy night."

Niekro's knuckleballs drove his catchers crazy; he holds the all-time record for wild pitches. They also drove hitters batty. One opponent, Bobby Murcer, said, "Hitting Niekro's knuckler is like eating jello with chopsticks."

Left to right: Bob Horner, Ralph Garr, Darrell Evans, Glenn Hubbard.

Like Spahn, Niekro played most of his years for poor Braves teams, so he had to win games on his own. Also like Spahn, he had his best years when the Braves needed him most. When Atlanta won its two National League Western Division crowns in 1969 and 1982, Niekro had records of 23–13 and 17–4, respectively.

He pitched until the age of forty-eight, and retired in 1987 with 318 victories and more than 3,300 strikeouts to his credit. Those numbers are sure to earn him a spot in the Hall of Fame with Warren Spahn and Hank Aaron.

Owner Ted Turner managed the Braves for one game—he lost to Pittsburgh, 2–1.

MURPHY'S A HERO ON AND OFF THE FIELD

As Hank Aaron was completing his final season in Atlanta in 1974, a young catcher named Dale Murphy was beginning his Braves career with the team's minor league club in Kingsport, Tennessee. By 1978, he was a regular on the big league club. Soon, Braves management decided that he was not cut out to be a catcher. Because of Murphy's speed and strong throwing arm, he was moved to center field.

The experiment paid off magnificently. In his first year as an outfielder (1980), Murphy boomed thirty-three home runs, had eighty-nine RBI, and was chosen for the All-Star team at his new position. In 1982 and 1983, Murphy was named the National League's Most Valuable Player. Only three other National Leaguers have ever won back-to-back MVP awards. Murphy led Atlanta to the National League Western Division title in his first MVP season and to a close second-place finish the following year. He was Atlanta's brightest star throughout the 1980s, until he was traded to the Philadelphia Phillies in 1990.

Dale Murphy (pages 26–27).

1 9 8 8

Rookie righthander Pete Smith compiled an impressive 2.27 ERA in 14 starts after the All-Star break.

Whether in Atlanta or Philadelphia, Dale Murphy has not only been great on the field, he has been an even bigger hero off it. A national sports magazine named him as one of its "Athletes Who Care" in a special poll. Murphy spends most of his free time raising money for charities, visiting hospitals, or working on special programs to encourage children to read better and stay in school. During one recent spring training, Murphy received more than fifty requests for his help. Exhausted by his double role as baseball player and humanitarian, Murphy turned down *one* of those requests. Five minutes later, he called up the charity and said he had changed his mind and would be available to do what he could to help.

Why does Dale Murphy do so much? "One of the most striking memories of my childhood," he says, "was my mother's going to school every day as a volunteer to teach handicapped children. When I asked her why she did it, she said, 'It's important.' Nothing more needed to be said. Society is what we make of it, so we'd better try to make it the best we can."

NEW STARS IN THE NINETIES

Since Dale Murphy was traded away from the Braves in 1990, Atlanta has begun turning to some of its young talent to move the team up in the Western Division standings. "We've been watching the young kids on our squad and in our farm system," manager Bobby Cox said, "and we think they're coming along just fine."

These youngsters include speedy outfielders Oddibe McDowell and Ron Gant, infielder Jeff Treadway, and the

1 9 9 0

*Infielder Jim Presley
(left) was acquired
by the Braves in a
trade with Seattle on
January 24.*

lefty-righty pitching combination of Tom Glavine and John Smoltz. Will they be another Warren Spahn and Lew Burdette?

One scouting report notes, "Glavine is a workhorse who'll put in at least thirty good starts a year. How many he wins, however, will depend on how much support his teammates give him."

When Smoltz was at the Triple A level, a top baseball magazine noted, "He's got the best arm in the league and is sure to be a top major league prospect." Smoltz proved that forecast correct when he was chosen to the National League All-Star team in 1989 at age twenty-two, the youngest Braves pitcher ever given that honor.

The pitching is in place, but what about the power? The Braves are counting on veterans such as Nick Esasky, Ernie Whitt, and Jim Presley to take advantage of "the

Pitcher John Smoltz.

Outfielder Ron Gant. 31

1 9 9 1

Led by pitcher John Smoltz the Braves were one of the up-and-coming teams in the National League.

launching pad" at Atlanta-Fulton County Stadium—if they stay healthy. Unfortunately, all three were injured during 1990.

Two of the Braves' most remarkable and unexpected stars of the 1990s are Lonnie Smith and Greg Olson. Drug problems almost drove Smith from baseball, but in 1989 he made a fantastic comeback in Atlanta, batting .315 with twenty-one homers and twenty-five stolen bases— not bad for a thirty-three-year-old. How many more good years does he have in him? Smith is confident. "I'm planning to stay out of trouble, play hard, and dedicate myself to baseball," he said.

Olson knocked around in the minors for more than ten years before making the Braves' 1990 squad as a backup catcher. The thirty-year-old rookie became a starter because of injuries to the top two Atlanta catchers. He made the most of his chance, even earning a spot on the National League All-Star team. "Who would ever have believed this?" the wide-eyed Olson said, as he lined up alongside the other National League stars.

Olson's and Smith's turnarounds have convinced Atlanta fans that the Braves will rebound too. One favorite expression in Georgia is: "The South shall rise again." The city of Atlanta's growth during the past thirty years has proven that statement true. Atlanta baseball fans also like to say, "The Braves shall rise again." The Braves have previously won world championships in Boston and Milwaukee; now it's Atlanta's turn.